BIG KICKS

Bob Kolar

WALKER BOOKS

IN A **QUIET LITTLE CORNER** of a busy little town lived a very large bear. His name was Biggie.

Biggie spent a lot of time by himself, playing jazz, eating peanut-butter-and-banana sandwiches and working on his amazing stamp collection.

One Saturday morning, there was a knock on Biggie's door.

It was the town football team.
"Hello," said Biggie. "How can I help you?"

"I can't ask him," said Chicken Rabbit. "I'm too afraid."
"I can't ask him," said Twirly Squirrel. "I'm too little."
"I can't ask him," said Smelly Smell Skunk. "I'm too stinky."
"I've forgotten what to ask him," said Fluff the Duck.
Poke the Turtle spoke up.

"We are the Mighty Giants," said Poke. "We have a big game today and Brown Dog has got fleas."

"We need someone with a big kick," said Twirly Squirrel.
"We need someone big and brave," said Chicken Rabbit.
"We need someone with a big brain," said Fluff the Duck.
"We need someone who doesn't stink," said Smelly Smell Skunk.

"We need a big bear!" they said together.

"But I've never played football before," said Biggie.

"Don't worry. You're big and the ball is little,"
 said Twirly Squirrel.
"Well, I do look good in red," said Biggie.
"Let's go!" said Chicken Rabbit.

The Screaming Pirates were warming up when the Mighty Giants arrived.

"This is Biggie," said Poke. "He's on *our* team."

"Hello," said Biggie.
"Uh-oh!" said the Pirates.

The game started with a big kick from Biggie.

But he missed the ball and landed on his bottom!
THUMP!

When Biggie tried to get to the ball, someone always got there first.
When Biggie tried to kick the ball, it always went the wrong way.
When Biggie tried to stop the ball, it always flew straight past him.

Maybe being big and being good at football were not the same thing.

The game was almost over and the score was tied.
Then something amazing happened.

Biggie saw a very rare, never-been-used, upside-down, limited-edition postage stamp!

He bent down to pick it up and ...

BONK!

The ball bounced off Biggie's head.

It bounced over his teammates.

It bounced around

the Screaming Pirates.

It bounced past the referee.

And, as time ran out, it bounced …

into the goal!

The Giants shouted, "We've won!"
The Pirates shouted, "We've lost!"

Biggie shouted, "I've found a
very rare, never-been-used,
upside-down, limited-edition
postage stamp!"

The team tried to carry Biggie off the field –
but they couldn't.

"I want to go home," said Biggie.
"It's time for a party!" cheered Chicken Rabbit.
"I have to add this to my collection," said Biggie.
"Party at Biggie's house!" shouted Fluff the Duck.

"What about food?" asked Poke the Turtle.
"What about music?" asked Twirly Squirrel.
"What are you going to do with a stinky old
postage stamp?" asked Smelly Smell Skunk.

"Follow me..." said Biggie.

Biggie threw a great party.
They ate peanut-butter-and-banana sandwiches,
played jazz and told exciting stories about football
and stamp collecting.

Now Biggie goes to every game.
He's still a special part of the team –
he's the Mighty Giants' biggest fan.